A PINCH OF DUST

Carol Buchanan

Carol Buchanan Books
Kalispell, Montana

Copyright © 2020 by Carol Buchanan. Second Edition.

All rights reserved. No part of this publication may be reproduced, distributed or transmitted in any form or by any means, including photocopying, recording, or other electronic or mechanical methods, without the prior written permission of the publisher, except in the case of brief quotations embodied in critical reviews and certain other noncommercial uses permitted by copyright law. For permission requests, write to the publisher at the address below.

Carol Buchanan Books
280 – 4th Ave WN
Kalispell, Montana 59901
https://carol-buchanan.com

Publisher's Note: This is a work of fiction. Names, characters, places, and incidents are a product of the author's imagination. Locales and public names are sometimes used for atmospheric purposes. Any resemblance to actual people, living or dead, or to businesses, companies, events, institutions, or locales is completely coincidental.

Book Layout ©2013 BookDesignTemplates.com

A Pinch of Dust / Carol Buchanan. – 2nd ed.
ISBN: 9781481072489

Acknowledgements

Thank you to all readers whose comments, opinions, and reviews brighten my life and show me the way to do the best work I can and to keep growing as a writer.

Dedication

In Loving Memory
Marilyn Ulleland
(December 13, 1931 – May 27, 2012)
Gracious older sister and chief encourager of my writing.
I miss you.

And the King will answer and say to them, "Assuredly, I say to you, inasmuch as you did it to one of the least of these My brethren, you did it to Me."

MATTHEW 25:40 NKJV

1. Janey

Clutching the lapels of her coat across her thin chest with one red, chapped hand, the child held out her other hand. "Mister, you got a pinch of dust to spare?" The coat was too large, and buttoned on the wrong side for a female. It was a small man's jacket, Daniel Stark supposed, in a threadbare summer wool too light to be anyone's winter garment. She looked to be any age between ten and thirteen and out of proportion thin and small for her age.

"Little girl, if I tried to pour a pinch of dust for you, it would all blow away." A dust devil blew snow in a miniature tornado that sent a man's hat skittering along the street. The owner ran after it. Just as he swooped down to grab the hat, the wind snatched it in a different direction. Men watching through the window of Fancy Annie's saloon laughed at his antics, though most people who had to be out on a day like this paid no attention. They butted head down into the wind, in a hurry to be home again, bumped into Dan without saying,

"Excuse me," as though blaming him for being an obstacle in their path.

"We gotta eat, mister." The little girl held her hand out and stood, feet apart, blocking his path. He sensed that she, like the wind, would be in his way no matter where he stepped.

They stood near the doorway to Miller's Dress Shop, midway down the slope of Wallace Street. Dan said, "Tell you what. Let's go in here and talk about this. It's too cold and windy to conduct business out of doors." As he spoke, a plan was forming, a strategy, like a hunt for criminals, except his Vigilante days were behind him, and neglecting children was no crime in the eyes of the law that he knew of. But who was this child? And who were her parents? Where were they, to let this waif beg money from strange men on the street?

"Do I get my dust?" Glaring at him, the little girl shifted her negligible weight, planting her feet more firmly on the board walk. She looked as if a strong gust would knock her over.

Who had taught this small female to brace grown-ups so fiercely? Why was she not at school with other children in the town? Could her parents not afford the $150 tuition? He thought of his stepdaughter who would shortly hurry home after school to make Christmas decorations from red paper spangled with gold flakes and tiny particles of gold known to a mining community as gold dust, or simply dust. After Christmas they would either save the decorations for next year or burn them, then pan the ashes to retrieve the gold. Dotty was about the same age as this child, and every time she came down to Wallace Street she parked herself in front of Miller's windows to sigh over the "pretties," as she called the ladies' dresses and assorted accessories. This girl, Dan felt certain, had never dared to wish for any of it.

How did she come to be begging on the street? Her parents ought to be shot for neglecting this brave little creature. He held the door to the dress shop open for her. "One thing's certain, young woman, you will get nothing if you refuse to step in here out of the wind."

"Can't eat no fancy duds," she said. Nevertheless, she stepped into the light and warmth of the shop, out of the darkening winter afternoon. She wore a pair of man's laced brogans on her feet. Good enough footwear when they were new, sturdy workman's shoes a man could wear to cross a continent without wearing them out. They looked as if they had done just that, with never a bit of polish or care. Like the girl herself.

Following her, he closed the door behind them with a no-nonsense thump just short of slamming it.

He paid no heed to the ladies whose chattering dried with their entrance. He fished a notebook out of his inner coat pocket and tore off a paper.

"What're you doin with that? I cain't spend no paper." She turned toward the door, her gaze following the passersby as they hurried about their errands. To him she seemed torn between staying here to see what might come of this, or trying her luck outside. Between landing the fish she had hooked, or dipping her line in a new stream. Between staying in the warmth, or going out again into the cold. She looked around him at the women openly watching them, whose staring jabbed at Dan through his heavy wool coat.

He brought out his pouch made of soft pale deer hide, called a poke in this gold mining country. "You need something to carry your dust in." He loosened the deer hide drawstring. "But I want something first." The watching women gasped, the sound like a puff of wind through pine needles.

"Sure, mister, why not you? Everybody else wants somethin."

Her face took the cynical pout he had seen on the faces of women who worked at Fancy Annie's. Did that look begin as early as this? "I want information."

"I don't know nothin."

That, he said to himself, was obvious. "What is your name?"

"Janey."

"It's not polite to call a lady by her first name on such brief acquaintance. What is your last name?"

She tilted her head, and a crease appeared between her brows. "Osborne. What do you need to know that for, anyway?"

"As I said, Miss Osborne, I'm trading information for dust. Where are your parents?"

"Mama died on the way out here, and Papa plays cards at the Nugget Saloon."

"I think I know of your father. Is his name Jordan Osborne?"

Behind him, an indignant snort came from the women. He guessed their outrage at him for befriending a gambler's spawn. The child's face reddened, and her chin quivered, but no tears came to her eyes, which narrowed at him or at the women behind him. "That's him. You lose money playin cards with him?"

"No. I've not had the pleasure of a game at his table." He tugged at his hatbrim. "My name is Daniel Stark, Miss Osborne." She did not offer her hand.

He smoothed the paper out on the top of a display case that held ostrich plumes and ribbons and glittery gewgaws women used to decorate their hats. Stretching out the mouth of his poke, he poured a small amount of dust onto the paper. Janey stood close to see what he did, and he caught the sour odor of long unwashing, as if cleanliness were a habit she had forgotten in the struggle simply to stay alive. Most people washed seldom or never during the winter; it took too long to heat water from ice or melted snow, and in the deep cold of a winter in Montana Territory, getting wet meant risking pneumonia. This, however, was a different odor; the mother had not taught her daughter how to care for herself at certain times.

Trickling onto the paper, the gold glistened in the lamplight. "Ooooh," the child said, "will you look a that?"

When he judged he had enough, he pulled the drawstring tight and replaced the poke in his front trousers pocket. Then he twisted the paper to hold the dust. "How many brothers and sisters have you?"

"They's six of us." Her eyes never left the paper, and when he still held onto it, she put out her small grimy paw.

"Six of you?" Dear God, Dan said to himself. This urchin was begging on the street to feed six mouths while her wastrel of a father spent his time gambling in saloons, and no doubt drinking up his winnings. A decent man would quit the damn cards and take an honest job that let him feed his family. There were good jobs in Virginia City, men working claims could earn three dollars a day. If he had not the physique for such hard labor he might clerk in a store at two dollars a day. Not as thrilling as the risks of 5-card stud, or, God help him, faro. But work paid the bills. Fed the children.

At cards, a man might go days waiting for his luck to turn from bad to good. He could wait forever, too, like Father... .

"Mister? Mister Stark?" The shrill voice jolted Dan out of his memory. "You givin that to me or just holdin it?"

Putting on his hat, he said, "I'm banking it for you. Come along."

She followed him out the door, protesting all the way. "You cain't do that. If you're a givin it to me, then give it, but don't put it where I cain't feed the young'uns with it."

The wind, carrying more snow, keened around corners. "Keep behind me," he told the child. "We're not going far." The wind pressed them from in front and Dan drove into it, head lowered. A board tumbled end over end down the street, and a horse shied, dumping its rider, who got up yelling at the animal. Dan pressed on, thinking the child would follow if she wanted her dust. To be sure, he looked over his shoulder to see the determined figure close in his wake.

She was still there, though he walked fast, when he reached Kiskadden's Stone Block, one of the few two-story buildings in Virginia City. He could never pass it without remembering the Vigilante meetings in the upper half-story. Next door to Kiskadden's, Dan stopped at the Eatery, a restaurant owned by his wife's friend, Lydia Hudson, a Quaker who did not much like him. Or any of the Vigilantes, for that matter. She didn't hold with violence, she had said. Often.

"Here we are." He pushed the door open. When the girl hesitated, he put a hand to her back and guided her ahead of him, squirming and shouting, "No! No!" into the restaurant. The wind slammed the door behind them. "We can't afford no rest'rants!" she shouted.

As he had hoped, it was still too early for customers, so he would be able to close this business with Mrs. Hudson in privacy. In the back of the single room, a big pot of stew bubbled on the cook stove. The smell made his mouth water.

Mrs. Hudson called out, "I can't leave this. Do thee come on back here." A short, stout woman, she was a widow whose husband had been killed in an accident shortly before their westward journey began. She always wore dresses of unrelieved black, their severity made less by the ruffles and jets sewn on the bodice, but aside from the decoration, they were so alike in cut that he occasionally wondered if she owned just one dress. One of these days he would ask Martha. Now she looked him up and down, and he thought in the dim light that her eyes widened when she saw the child.

"What have we here?" asked Mrs. Hudson.

"A failure of fatherhood," Dan said.

Janey shook her head, "No, he ain't. He tries hard, but this place is too —"

As if she had not spoken, Dan went on, "He's Jordan Osborne, a gambler at the Nugget Saloon. This young woman is Janey Osborn, the eldest of six. She goes by Janey. The mother died on the road out here."

"And thee brought her here?" By the tone of her voice, Mrs. Hudson was not pleased. Gamblers were riffraff, and respectable Christian folk did not associate with them.

"Along with this." Dan handed her the twist of paper. "There's enough to feed Miss Osborne and her younger brothers and sisters – six in all – for perhaps a week. After that, let me know if you need more gold. But I want all of them to eat and eat well."

If he had expected the child to thank him, he would have been mistaken, because she flung about to scream at him. "No, no, no! That's my gold. You were givin it to me! You don't give it to her. You don't give it to nobody but me. You can't —"

Dan cut into her diatribe. "And would you feed your brothers and sisters? Or would you give it to your father? And would he use it to feed you, or would it be his next stake?"

By her silence he knew the answer. "That's precisely why I'm giving it to Mrs. Hudson. She will hold it for you and use it only to feed you and your brothers and sisters. You bring them here to eat, and she will give you good food."

When Janey would have said more, and none of it good, judging by her stubborn pout, Mrs. Hudson said, "Thank Mr. Stark, Janey. Thee and thy brothers and sisters do not have to be hungry again as long as thee are in Virginia City."

"I wanted Papa to feed us." Tears broke through and flowed down her face. Her nose ran. She wiped her face on the coat sleeve. "I was going to give it to him and make him feed us."

Mrs. Hudson said, "What does he do with the dust thee gives him, my dear?"

Sniffs and sobs were her only answer. Over the little girl's head, Mrs. Hudson met Dan's eyes. "He drinks it away?" she asked, her voice barely audible through the girl's crying. She gathered the child to her and let her sob into her apron-covered bosom.

"Or gambles it, no doubt," said Stark.

"Dear Lord, what a world this is." Mrs. Hudson patted the child's quivering back. "What will thee do now?"

In Dan's mind an idea was taking shape. "I think I'll see about putting a stop to this."

Janey twisted around, fear flared in her eyes. She cried out over Mrs. Hudson's reprimand; together they fired a volley of words at him: "Oh, mister, don't hurt him," and "There is no need for such action."

2. The Plan

His fingers ached from cold even through his fur-lined leather gloves, and cold air rasped in his throat through the twice-wrapped wool muffler. Only his eyes looked out between it and his hat brim. Anyone meeting him might assume he was after their gold, bundled up like one of the murderous gang of armed robbers and conspirators he and the other Vigilantes had hanged last winter. That was what Mrs. Hudson had referred to: hanging the members of that murderous conspiracy. What would she have had them do instead, in this country of no laws? Should they have let the mayhem continue? He knew the answers as well as he knew his name, though voices whispered questions and men swung in his nightmares.

He climbed the slope on Wallace Street. Hardly anyone this morning was out; he nodded to the few passersby, grateful that none wanted to stand in the cold and talk any more than he did. He left buildings behind, and the street became a snow-filled suggestion amid the sagebrush. Still he pressed on, breathing through the muffler, whose wool hairs clung to his lips. The cold bit into his feet through the heavy soles of his boots and thick wool socks. Yet he could not go back to sit in his office, where even his sparse furniture left little room to pace. He had to walk, to wrestle down the voices and remembered stench of men dying, make room in his mind to keep company with an idea, let it emerge, turn it into a plan. His heart beat faster. The snow squeaked under his boots in a rhythm that matched his heartbeat. When he turned back toward town, he had turned the idea into a plan.

Janey Osborne's father was a gambler, was he? His daughter begged on the streets, did she? Thank God she had not turned to something worse, though it was not through her father's guidance that she had not. He had to be taught a lesson, to learn what was important in his life, in the one way he might understand. What if he lost everything at poker?

Dan's boot heels beat on the wood planks of the board walk. He could do it. Risky, yes. Who else, though, could beat a gambler at his own game except another gambler? Who else could help the Osborne children? He would do it. For the Osborne children, for the sake of his own child now on the way, and for Martha's youngsters, he would do it. He would take Osborne on and beat him at his own game.

Between one step and the next, the terrible uncertainty of poker drove at him. Winning was only a possibility. He might win. No more than that. If the cards fell right. If he had the patience to wait. If he did not plunge, as Father had done, and at last, having lost everything – his own fortune and clients' money – and having stripped three generations of his own family of everything, leaving them dependent on the kindness of the Church, he had shot himself. Left his eldest son to clean up the mess.

He was too much his father's son. He knew what it was to lose big at poker, a game he had learned to play while he was barely out of dresses, when Father had taught him to count so he could learn 5-card stud. He could not promise himself – or Martha – he would not lose. Poker broke more promises than miners broke bones. He had lost a gold claim at poker.

Unlike Father, though, he would not risk the family.

First, he must tell Martha.

3. Martha

Before he had the chance to finish telling his wife what he planned, Martha grasped his intention. Plainly, she did not like it. Her eyes, that he often thought of as 'luminous,' shone a different light on his intention. When she was upset, her Appalachian hill accent came back, taking over pronunciation and grammar that she forgot to correct as she usually did. "Why d'you got to take such a misbegotten chance on them no-account young'uns?" Sitting in her upholstered rocking chair next to a potbelly stove in their reading corner, she clutched her hands around the mountain of her belly, big with his child, her knuckles showing pale and yellowish.

"Because Janey begs on the street while her father gambles and drinks up his winnings in the Nugget Saloon. Because Christmas is here. Because those children are nearly starving." He kept his voice gentle, thinking of Dotty, who already turned men's heads, with her long blond hair, her budding figure. Someday, not so far off, she would be what was known as "statuesque," and he would have a father's proper duty of guarding her from the wrong kind of suitors. Who would guard Janey? Her father? He seriously doubted it. "Janey Osborne faces a frightening future. I doubt she has ever gone to school, or had proper guidance, except perhaps when her mother lived, though certainly not from her father." After a pause while Martha's lips remained a thin line, he added, "We have enough gold that we can spare something for them." Perhaps she should have educated her about how much money he had made trading gold in New York, in the Gold Room, but considering everything, the less he said about his overlong stay in his home city, the better.

"Then why not just give them more? You don't need to be taking chances like that. You could lose. You lost a claim before."

He winced. He hated to be reminded of losing his claim. "I don't always lose. I've won, too."

"But you don't know, do you? Nobody knows if they'll win or lose at cards, or horse races, or what fish will bite next."

"No, I can't promise not to lose. Poker is not a game of promises. We never know what cards we'll be dealt. Don't ask me for a promise I can't keep."

"Then I can't give you a blessing on this, even for a good cause. It can only have a bad outcome, and you know it. It was all right when you was single, but you ain't single no more. You have us to look after – me, and this young'un —" patting her belly "— and Dotty and Timothy. You done took us on, and you made us promises, not just to me, but to them, too. And now you'll do this? We had one gambler to worry us. I thought you'd be different."

A knife could not cut so deep. Her first husband had been a bully and a drunk as well as a gambler. Many of the Vigilantes had suspected him of being one of the gang that had plagued the area last winter.

Silent, he quelled the first urge to walk away from her, because he did not know where it might lead him, out of the house, perhaps out of town, out of the Territory. Perched on a wooden kitchen chair in front of her, he sat knee to knee. Her comfortable chair had been moved as close as safety allowed to the stove. These days, bearing as she was, she was often cold. His own easy chair stood empty at the other side of a round table holding a lamp and their books. Her only book *The Holy Bible*, while Wilkie Collins's mystery, *The Woman in White,* lay on top of his bound volume of *The Atlantic Monthly*.

Studying his hands, lost between the urge to leave and the need to win her over to his idea, he could think of nothing to say. He was at a loss, he who could figure instant by instant when to sell short by calculating the premium against the rapid-fire rise and fall of gold values. He, who could track a deer through a forest by its occasional hoof print, or a tuft of fur on a broken twig. But into an emotional swamp he could not venture. And as he sat helpless and silent, she rescued him.

"Why do you have to do this? Tell me that at least. Why are you putting those young'uns against your own?"

It was a question he had not asked himself, so how could he tell her? He had not the words to tell her how the sight of his mother and younger brothers and sisters leaving their house forever had torn at his heart. Yet they, and Martha and her children, and his own coming child, would never suffer the fate of Janey Osborne. It was a man's duty to protect the helpless, or why had God made him bigger and stronger?

"I need to know, Dan'l. Or what's to become of you and me?" Her voice trembled and broke.

He looked up, and saw tears in her eyes. It struck him with the strength of a revelation: she was as frightened as he. That sudden realization startled him into speaking, telling her something he had never said even to himself, and certainly not what he had been thinking at all.

"To balance the hangings."

She knew all about him being the Vigilante prosecutor, how they had hanged 24 men, and how five graves lay atop the hill on the north side of Daylight Creek. She knew how the dead men's friends insisted loud and long that they were not guilty, that the Vigilantes – he and the others – were the murderers. It would have been impossible to keep it from her, when his nightmares woke them both. What if among them, one or two were as innocent as they claimed, despite the evidence?

"You did the right thing," Martha said. "You and the others. Y'all made Alder Gulch safe for families, and I won't have no one sayin different." She reached for his hands, and he inched forward on the chair to clasp them.

"I have to do this other thing, though. Jordan Osborne can't be allowed to sacrifice his —" Breaking off, he stared at her. "So that's it. You're afraid I'm ready to sacrifice you and our three for them. That will not happen."

She did not seem to hear the last statement. "Ain't I been telling you just that very thing in plain words? You're about to risk the dust we need to live on for them no-account young'uns." Jerking back her hands, she folded them across her stomach again, and closed her lips, narrowed her eyes.

"Never. I'll carry a stake in a poke, and when that's gone, I'm out of the game. I promise."

"How big a stake?"

"Four ounces. Seventy-two dollars." The exchange rate of gold in Virginia City was eighteen dollars an ounce.

"We can afford to lose that much?"

He had not told her he had brought back a fortune – thousands of dollars – from New York, all in Double Eagles and greenbacks. Not trusting banks, he had divided it and hidden it here and there so that if thieves found one part they would not find it all. "We can afford it. I know it's a lot of money, but we have enough to venture this for a good cause."

At last she nodded. "All right. If'n you say so. Just bring back that four ounces. They can have the rest." He was rising to his feet when she asked, "When do you plan to do this?"

"Tonight."

"Tonight? You'll gamble in a saloon on Christmas Eve? You'll be sitting in the seat of the ungodly when the Lord come?"

"I want those children to have a Christmas they'll remember. If they never have another decent Christmas, they'll have this one to look back on."

"Timothy and Dotty need you here for Christmas. Your first obligation is to us."

"I'll make it as short a game as I can. I'll be home soon."

"You putting them riff-raff young'uns ahead of your own. It ain't right."

When he would have kissed her, she turned her face away from him.

4. Dotty and Timothy

Voices mumbled through the wall of the office next door. Somewhere along the veranda attached to the outside wall of the office building a door slammed, and footsteps crept gingerly down the stairs to Jackson Street below. His office was so cold that a thin skin of ice had formed in the water pitcher while he was out, and the fire, which he had banked for safety before he left, had nearly died. He crouched down to shovel the ashes at the bottom of the pot-bellied stove (as tall as he was) into a bucket. A yell from outside, and something heavy crashed and rumbled down the stairs. Why had Solomon Content built in this country of deep winters without an inside staircase to the second floor offices? Forgetting that he held the bucket of ashes, he ran outside.

Below, a heavy man knelt amid the snow swirling about him. Other men helped him up and supported him down the slope toward Wallace Street. Remembering the ashes, Dan backed down the steps one at a time, scattering ashes across each step as he went. He had walked up three or steps with the empty bucket when he heard behind him a girl's light step among the heavier trudge of a man's boots down the slope. Nearing the top of the stairs, he heard the girl call his name. His stepchildren, Timothy and his young sister, Dorothy, stood at the bottom of the stairs.

"Come on up," he called to them. "It's too cold to stand out here." By the time they entered his office, he had laid a new fire on the embers of the old and stood ready with flint and steel. Just in case the embers did not ignite the old fire.

Both the children took after their natural father in physique, being tall for their ages and blond. At twelve, Dotty did not yet pin up her hair, and it cascaded down her back in bright golden waves from under her blue knitted hat. Timothy's blond hair fell past his ears; he had the miner's dislike of wasting time away from the claim, although his mother had nagged at him to get it cut for Christmas.

Tomorrow.

Though he brought up chairs for them by the stove, they planted themselves in front of him, and did not sit down. The top of Dotty's head came to his breastbone, and Timothy looked up at him from the level of his chin.

Timothy, as usual, spoke for them both, his chin thrust out, his fists balled at his sides. "Mam told us what a damn fool scheme you've thought up." His sister gasped at the swear word. "What do you want to go and do that for?" The words all rushing together: "whaddayayouwannagoandothatfor? "Tonight of all nights?"

"Didn't your mother explain it? I'm taking four ounces of dust as a stake, and I promised her I wouldn't use more." He looked from one to the other, fixed them with a glare. Without him, they would be in the Osborne children's predicament, and did they begrudge these other children a helping hand when they now had so much? "Jordan Osborne is doing to his children what your father did to you. What my father did to his children. I aim to stop him."

"What if you don't?" demanded Timothy. "What if your scheme backfires?"

Dan nodded, pretended to a calm he did not feel. "There's always that chance. Just like in mining. There's always a chance a claim will be worthless. Or the value of gold will drop instead of rise. I think I'm a better player than he is." The fire had a good start now. He closed flint and steel in the tinder box and stowed it in a pocket.

"You should be home with us, instead of playing poker."

"I'm doing this to help the Osborne children." The warmth from the stove could not yet cut the ice on the windows. In the next room, men argued, their voices growing louder.

Tim snorted. "Mam said you wouldn't change your mind, though we might try as hard as we could." He removed a glove and reached into an inner coat pocket. Drawing out a folded piece of paper, he held it out toward Dan. "You care more for them no-account brats than you do for your own family." Thrusting the paper at Dan, he said, "Here. Take it. Mam wrote you a note."

It was perhaps the first note she had ever written in her life, certainly the first he had ever received from her. He broke the thumb-print in candle-wax she had put on it for a seal and unfolded it. Twisting so as to catch the best light from the window over his desk, he read it, his eyes growing moist. There was no salutation, and the ink had blotted where she had stopped and rested the pen point on the paper, to think, perhaps. She formed her letters like a schoolchild, but the sight of their laborious shapes filled his heart; a year ago she had been the abused, illiterate wife of a drunken bully.

> I couldn't stop Timothy and Dotty. Come home soon. Good luck. God bless.

Blinking against his own rising emotions, he said, "Your mother is the bravest person I know." He gave them the paper to read. "I don't claim to be much of a Christian, but I do know that those who have more must share with those who have less."

4. The Game

The stake weighed heavy in his pocket and the beer glass chilled his hand. Thick, creamy foam trailed a sunlit, earthy smell of hops down the side of the glass. A hunter pretending no interest in his quarry, he drifted among the poker tables while the blood ran faster in his veins. From the sides of his eyes he watched the table where Osborne sat, his side whiskers drooping down his jaw, shoulders squared and back straight. The man probably thought his posture was a good imitation of confidence. Occasionally, he stretched his neck to the left before reaching out to the pot and laying down a chip. At those times, he bet from a weak hand, or one with an ace up card, and twice he won the pot with a high card. He seemed to have faith in high cards.

Another player caught Dan's interest. A darkhaired man tossed out a chip with a negligent flick of his wrist when he thought he had a good hand, but he didn't seem to prefer any one sort of bet over another. Dan wiped the back of his hand across his mouth. The fellow favored pairs. Unless he had a pair, he folded after the third deal. He would not wait beyond that to see a pair turn into three of a kind.

Just when he decided he had enough of their tells in his memory, the dark-haired man waited out the entire hand, even though he lost. Watch out for monkey wrenches, he told himself, easing closer to be ready. When the game broke up, he asked, as if he did not know, "What's the game?"

"Five-card stud," replied the dark-haired man. "Aces high, dollar bets, five-dollar limit. Penny ante, you ask me."

A rich game to most men in Virginia City, where a high wage was three dollars a day. Yet this man called it penny ante. The most dangerous kind, that bled a man dry before he knew it. As he hesitated, wanting not to seem too eager, Osborne looked up, his brown eyes as mournful as a hound's, though a smile bent his lips upward at the corners. "Want to sit in? We're going to be short a couple of players."

"Take my chair." A small man scraped back his chair from the table and stood up. "It may be penny ante to him, but it's too rich for me. I'm going home. It's Christmas Eve, after all. I'd rather spend it with my family than here."

Almost, he followed the man from the saloon; almost, he took his hand from the chair and left his beer. Remember the mission, he reminded himself as he settled in at the table with his best affable manner. He said his name, received the others' names. On his right, between him and Osborne, was a thin man called Martin. Then Osborne, with the drooping whiskers. Then came the dark-haired man, Beaumont, who looked like he smelled something bad, perhaps the Irishman on his right, who exaggerated his brogue like a turn in a show. Dan doubted his name was Doyle; it was too convenient. Next came Vasquez, the Mexican who probably spoke and understood better English than he let on. Most people with little English watched Anglos carefully, but Vasquez looked no one in the eye. A man named Lawson, who sat on Dan's left, gave him a minimal nod.

To each he murmured, "Glad to know you," offered his hand to shake, noted Martin's too-long lingering clasp, Osborne's sweaty palm, Beaumont's hard dominating grip. Lawson's hand lay limp in his own before withdrawing. Vasquez held up a bandaged right hand, shrugged while looking at Dan's chin.

"High card starts the betting." Beaumont shuffled the cards two or three times, straightened them, and stroked an edge with his thumb. "Here." He gave the deck to Doyle to cut. "I'll deal for high card."

As he dealt, Dan said, "We should make the game more interesting." To himself, he thought, *Forgive me, Martha, but the four-ounce stake will be safe.*

"I'll say." Beaumont did not miss a deal; his hands moved as if with a will of their own, and a card sailed to a landing in front of each man. "What do you-all think?"

Lawson coughed into a handkerchief. "Fine with me." He thumped a fist against his chest. "Damn cold air in this country. I didn't get out in time."

Pointing at the chip holder in front of him, Dan said, "So. White for a dollar, blue for five, yellow for ten? We each start with a hundred dollars."

Martin whistled between his front teeth. "That's pretty rich."

"Fine with me," said Osborne. "It's Christmas Eve. I want to get something nice for my littles."

A blank silence pressed on the table. Did every man want to tell Osborne what he thought? *If you want to do something for your 'littles' as you call them, get out of here. Buy them food. Pay the rent. Do your duty as a father.*

Looking around, perhaps wondering what the silence was about, Osborne said, "I'll stay."

Beaumont said, "Anyone out?"

Each man shook his head or mumbled that he was staying.

Dan said, "We're all in. Call it five ounces of dust to the hundred? Or five and a half?"

"Let's be keeping it simple for dunderheads like me," said Doyle. "Call it an even five or six."

"The exchange rate—" Dan started to say, and stopped when the others looked at him as if he spoke Greek. Doyle scratched his collarbone under his shirt. Dan was happy he did not sit next to him. If he got a bug, he couldn't sleep with Martha in their bed until he was clean again, a risky proposition in this cold weather. People who bathed in winter were known to catch pneumonia.

"Oh, hell," said Beaumont. "We won't bother with that. How about white for a half ounce, blue for an ounce, yellow for two ounces?"

"Fine," said Martin. "We can each start with five ounces. Okay with you boys?"

Osborne said, "Four white, four blue, and three yellow. That's seven ounces."

"We all good for it?" asked Beaumont.

"We better be." Martin laughed, a quick ha-ha without humor.

"And you?" A challenge rang in Beaumont's quiet voice.

"Yes." Dan had come out with enough gold dust to see his plan through, but now, in his determination not to leave any of it to Osborne, he added the promise to himself that Beaumont would not keep one flake.

The deal fell to Vasquez, who shuffled the deck twice. Lawson cut, and Vasquez shuffled it again. "Ante up," he said. "Uno white chip."

At other tables, men joked and laughed, and farther back in the long room someone played a reedy-sounding instrument for others singing counterfeit jolly Christmas songs. Dan tossed a white chip into the pot. When the first hole card landed, the room shrank to walls of shadow cast by the lamp hanging over the table and the eight players sitting around it.

His hole card was an ace of hearts, the second a four of clubs. Lawson, with a ten of spades, checked. Everyone else did likewise. On the third deal, Vasquez dealt Dan a seven of hearts and a second ten to Lawson, who opened with a bet of $25. Dan folded, as did the others. Lawson scooped up the chips and left them in front of himself. He put on a satisfied smile.

Dan glanced at Osborne. How did this man think to raise his children? How could he not provide for them? A man with children, a father, who let his daughter beg on the streets. Had he failed to learn the same lessons Father had failed at? Never bet more than you can afford to lose. Fold even a good hand when you suspect an opponent has a better one. Never stay with losing cards in hopes that the next deal will turn one of them into a winner. Stay cool under pressure. Feeling someone's stare creeping over him as if he had caught a louse, he glanced around. Beaumont watched him. He met Beaumont's stare with a silent challenge, knowing he now had two enemies in this game.

His hole card was a two of spades. He remembered other games, other times that a pair of two's had made a winning hand, but he dropped his gaze to watch for the first up card. It was an ace. Mindful of the two, he was relieved when Martin checked, despite his queen of diamonds up card, and the checks ran around the table. So Martin was smart enough not to open, because what fool would bet a queen against an ace? Checking and betting the minimums, the game ran to the fifth card with everyone still in, and gave Dan a second ace. With a sigh of regret, he bet the maximum. He knew the size of the bet did not matter; everyone would fold no matter what.

A modest pile of chips lay in front of him. The game rolled on, the cards slapped down, men bet, checked, called, now and then raised, more often folded. The pile of chips grew, but too slowly. Once or twice the men broke to get another beer, or went outside to relieve themselves, and the smoke lay under the lamp in stagnant air fragrant with the thick smell of beer.

The cards fell, the hands see-sawed back and forth, no one winning or losing much. The stacks of white chips in front of each man rose and sank and rose again, but their supplies of blue chips and yellow chips stayed constant.

Something would have to break soon, or he'd have to face Martha and the youngsters empty-handed when he came home tired and stinking.

Past midnight, faces had taken on a gray tinge, and everyone's eyes were red. Did they sting as much as his? Fishing out a handkerchief, he dabbed at them, inhaled the scent of wood smoke that made him think of Martha. He longed to be at home, beside her in their bed, his hand on her belly feeling the child move inside her.

Doyle quit, and they paused while Osborne cashed him out, putting the house cut into a separate poke. After another game, when Martin quit, taking with him a heavier poke, Dan stood up to loosen stiff muscles. When he sat down again, something in the air changed. The men who were left had a different set to their shoulders. They curled their hands around their hole cards to protect them with near-closed fists. Despite the empty beer glasses, no one went to the bar.

Osborne dealt. Receiving a jack of clubs for a hole card, Dan read the men's tells when his first up card fell: a six of diamonds. Beaumont, with a king of hearts that bested Lawson's king of diamonds, bet $25 with a confidence that told Dan his own jack of clubs had no chance, nor did his lowly six of spades. When the bet came to him, he folded. Beaumont pushed the betting ever higher as the players called and raised and called on nearly every card, and Dan watched until Beaumont won with his ace in the hole as high card. Clever, Dan thought, and filed the information at the front of his mind: Beaumont incited men to bet when he had a good hole card.

On the next deal Dan worked to keep his tells even as Vasquez dealt him a king of hearts in the hole followed by an ace. He floated a small bet that Lawson, Beaumont, and Vasquez rose to, telling him that Beaumont's hole card was probably an ace, and Lawson might have a king to pair the king he now held, and Vasquez's hole card could well be a jack, like Lawson's possible king, pairing the jack that now lay between his hands. The other two folded. On the third round, a king came to Dan, a jack settled in front of Beaumont, and Lawson, dealing himself an eight, folded. Beaumont's jacks were no problem, but an inner voice screamed at him: *Vasquez's hole card is an ace, fold while you can, don't get in deeper*, but Father's voice, coming for the first time, insisted, *Stick with it, son, hold on*. The betting went around, and the pot grew. Dan shooed away the screamer. Beaumont licked his lips as Lawson dealt him an ace. He did not smile, but his eyes lighted, and Dan knew the damn man had a pair of aces that beat his own pair of kings. Then Lawson dealt him another king. He now held three kings and an ace, and Beaumont opened with a $100 bet guaranteed to push both Vasquez and Dan into folding and give him the big pot.

Dan had a different idea. He called the hundred dollars and raised another hundred. Vasquez folded, and Beaumont called and raised, and Dan met him call for call and raise for raise. There was no one else in the room, the world did not exist beyond the lamplight though he had a sense of men breathing, muttering, and Osborne's eyes were as wide and startled as if he had never thought to see the like.

Beaumont called, and Dan said, "Let's see them."

Beaumont's hand fanned out across the table. As Dan had thought, the hole card was an ace. With a short laugh, the man reached out to take the pot. "I got you," he chortled.

"Not quite." Dan laid out his cards, hole card last. It didn't matter that he had three kings. Three two's would have done the same, because, as everyone in the room knew, three of a kind beats a pair.

"Oh, Christ." Beaumont slumped back in his chair. His hands dropped to his lap.

Osborne echoed him. "Jesus Christ."

"Yes," Dan said. "He was born today."

Vasquez crossed himself, murmuring in Spanish.

5. Christmas Shopping

The next morning, he awoke to muted sounds from the big room where the family lived during the day. Lying there, he listened to them. Dotty laughed, and Martha shushed her with the warning, "Dan'l came home late." Timothy's uneven voice rumbled, "In the saloons on Christmas Eve. That ain't right." He ended on a squeak. Martha hushed him, too. "He done what he set out to do." The youngsters came back as one, "He won? How much did he win?" Martha said, "He'll tell you about it when he gets up."

When he came out, the youngsters' frozen looks and tight lips would have withered him with shame if he had deserved their scorn. He laid his sack of winnings beside his plate at one end of the long oval table that served for a work table and eating table. "Merry Christmas," he said. He untied the knot and opened the sack. Taking out a poke, he hefted it twice in his hand. "Tim, give this to your mother." He tossed the poke to his stepson. "It's the stake. All the dust I took to gamble with." It gratified him to see how Martha clasped the poke in both hands, her face bright with a surge of pleasure. "The rest of it is for the Osborne children."

"Janey Osborne won't have to beg in the streets any more?" asked Dotty.

"That's right. At least, not after I've been around to some of the suppliers today." He knew, this being Virginia City, all the stores would be open, Christmas Day or not. The saloons, too.

While he ate his breakfast, they helped him write a list of supplies and clothes for the Osborne children. Dotty advised on pretties for Janey, Tim on boys' clothes and toys, and Martha added her recommendations about food. "Milk," she reminded him. "Especially make sure of the milk."

"Should I buy anything for Mr. Osborne?" he asked them.

They spoke nearly together: "No." "He don't deserve it. Wasn't for you, those young'uns would starve," Tim said. "He's been no shakes at all as a father."

For a moment he just smiled at them. Nor was yours, he told them silently. Even worse than mine, who taught me one useful thing: How to play poker. God help me, I will not be such a father to you – all of you, he added to himself, laying his hand on Martha's stomach, feeling his child kick within her.

Taking up the sack, he said, "I'm off to do some Christmas shopping. I'll be back before dinner."

6. Jordan Osborne

Even on Christmas Day, in less than two hours Dan had completed his shopping, made all his arrangements, and spent his winnings and something over.

He found Jordan Osborne slumped over a card table in the Nugget Saloon, snoring, his head pillowed on his folded arms. Had the man bothered to go home? Sitting opposite him, Dan slammed his open hand down on the table top. Osborne's head bounced. He snapped upright, befuddled from interrupted sleep and the alcohol still in his blood. Seeing Dan, he shook his head as though to clear it. He mumbled something. Dan said, "Speak up. I can't hear you."

"You. You robbed my littles."

"The hell I did. You did that yourself."

"How could I? I wanted to buy them a Christmas present."

"You did. Here are the receipts." From his inside coat pocket, Dan took out five pieces of paper, each one a receipt for accounts opened at the Pioneer Clothing Store, Dance & Stuart, Baume's Wholesale and Retail Grocers, the City Book Store, the Eatery. One by one, he laid them in front of Osborne as if he dealt a hand of stud. Each one of them had a credit amount sufficient for a family for a year. More, if they were careful, but children grew quickly.

"You did this?" Osborne's eyes filled with tears.

"Yes. I took my winnings and went shopping. Look closer, though. You'll see the receipts are all made out to Janey. The merchants all know to give her what she needs for herself and the younger ones. You won't get a pinch of dust out of this. Not even a flake. You don't deserve it. If Janey wants to share some of this, that's her business. But the merchants won't let her have any dust. They know she'd give it to you and you'd blow it here."

The gambler's hands rose to cover his face. "Oh, good Christ, have I sunk so low?"

"You know the answer to that question." Dan rose to his feet. "Now get up. You're going home to take these papers to your daughter."

"What will you do?" Osborne stood, picked up the receipts, put them in his notecase, and tucked it into his inside coat pocket.

"I'll be right behind you, watching your back."

7. Janey

The next day, the 26th, Dan sat in his office, making notes for a presentation he would give to the new Chief Justice for Montana Territory. It involved complex comparisons of law between the Common Law and the interim statutes governing the Territory, and he was to brief His Honor about the necessity of instituting the Common Law to govern mining uniformly throughout the Territory. The interim statutes mandated a different system for marking gold claims than most miners had used, and they were dead set against re-marking all of their claims over again. He and his client were to be in court by noon, and he was deep in thought when a knock at the outside door startled him. The morning sun silhouetted a young girl against the glass in the upper half of the door.

When he opened it, Janey Osborne walked over his mudsill to the stove, where she stood warming her outstretched hands. Dan closed the door behind her. "Janey! What brings you out in this weather? Won't you sit down?"

"I can't, Mr. Stark. We come to thank you. You gotta just see what you done for us." With that, she whistled a piercing blast between her front teeth.

Dan heard a thunder of small feet up the wooden steps. He opened the door to all of the Osborne children. They lined up in front of him like little troopers, stair-step fashion, presenting themselves for his inspection. The child next oldest to Janey held the baby. Each one wore a warm coat, mittens, hats, and stout winter boots, and the small round faces beamed like miniature suns. Best of all, Janey's face had lost its grey look of hunger, and the dark circles under her eyes had faded somewhat. Before Dan could speak, Janey stomped her left foot, and they chorused, "Merry Christmas, Mr. Stark, and thank you kindly."

"You're all very welcome, I'm sure. Janey, I'm happy to see you all looking so chipper, but I didn't do anything. Your father —"

Janey shook her head so hard her braid slapped one shoulder and then the other. "No, sir. When Papa came home yesterday, I saw you standing back a ways behind him. If he'd of won all that dust, we'd of never seen us a flake. He'd of drunk it all up. You done this, and we're all mighty grateful. Come spring, when the passes clear, though, we'll be leavin Virginia City. Papa's thinkin we can make a fresh start somewheres else, with nothing to remind him what he was."

8. Daniel

When the children had trooped out, calling "Merry Christmas" to him as they galloped heedlessly down the icy stairs, Dan stood at the door despite the cold to watch them skip along Jackson Street until they turned the corner onto Wallace, and their voices were lost in the snow-muted noise of the street – sleigh brakes squealing, horses neighing, men shouting to each other.

He closed the door. His office was colder. He stirred up the sinking fire in his stove and added three more quarter rounds of wood. He had to finish thinking through these legal issues in order to convince His Honor of the wisdom of doing the right thing by the mining interests he represented. But the ink dried on his pen as he sat lost in memories, gazing at the balance scales on his desk. It was several minutes later that he felt tears wetting his cheeks.

"Merry Christmas," he whispered. "Merry Christmas, Father."

Author's Note

Sometimes, during the past twenty years that I've been researching the history of Montana, primarily the Alder Gulch area in the southwestern part of the state, I've come across anecdotes about people that stay with me, biding their time until they are ready to become stories. *A Pinch of Dust* is based on one of those.

Martha Jane Canary (or Cannary), born May 1, 1852, as a girl of 14 begged on the streets of Virginia City and Nevada City while her widowed father gambled in the saloons. The oldest of six children, she and her younger brothers and sisters had lost their mother on the trip West not long before the family arrived in Virginia City in 1866.

On one cold, snowy day, dressed in a light summer-weight dress and carrying her youngest sister, an infant, she knocked on the door of James and Pamelia Fergus, who took pity on her and helped her and her siblings. They also became instrumental in making sure all the poor amidst the enormous wealth of the gold region were not forgotten.

After spending the winter of 1866-1867 in Virginia City, the family moved on. John Canary, the father, took up farming and settled down to tend his crops and his family. He died within a year. Again, Martha Jane took responsibility for them all, taking on whatever work she could find, until in 1874 she became a scout for the Army.

Though she never learned to read or write, she gained fame – some would say notoriety – as Calamity Jane. She cultivated the tough exterior that was a lone woman's best defense in wild places, earning her nickname, by some accounts, because she warned men that to cross her was to "court calamity."

Calamity Jane died August 1, 1903.

Like This Story?

Read more about the Vigilantes of Montana!

Daniel Stark found a family in a situation much like that of the Osbornes when he went to the Montana gold fields in 1863. His mission: to get enough gold to recoup the fortune his father had lost to gambling before he shot himself. Because of armed robbers that infest the roads, he realizes that if he tries to leave Alder Gulch with his gold, he will not survive to take it home.

God's Thunderbolt: The Vigilantes of Montana Winner of a 2009 Spur award from the Western Writers of America.

https://www.amazon.com/Gods-Thunderbolt-Vigilantes-Montana-Vigilante-ebook/dp/B0028AD8UE/ref=sr_1_1?keywords=god%27s+thunderbolt%3A+the+vigilantes+of+montana&qid=1571352668&s=books&sr=1-1

The Devil in the Bottle: the Tragedy of Joseph "Jack" Slade. Joseph Slade has been a hero to the town of Virginia City, but he is a binge drinker who goes on rampages that threaten to destroy the town, as he destroyed Denver. How can the Vigilantes stop him? He has committed no capital offense

https://www.amazon.com/Devil-Bottle-Tragedy-Montana-Vigilante/dp/0986420336/ref=sr_1_1?keywords=the+devil+in+the+bottle%3A+the+tragedy+of+Joseph+%22Jack%22+Slade&qid=1571352784&s=books&sr=1-1

Gold Under Ice. 2011 Spur Finalist. Dan Stark takes his gold home to pay his father's debts, but discovers that because of fluctuating exchange rates, he does not have enough gold to satisfy the Bank of New York. Before he can return to Alder Gulch, and Martha, he must repay the debt. But how can he get enough gold? If he becomes a gold trader, he could lose everything and incur the wrath of President Lincoln himself.

https://www.amazon.com/Gold-Under-Vigilante-Quartet-Book-ebook/dp/B003XVZAAS/ref=sr_1_1?keywords=gold+under+ice&qid=1571352838&s=books&sr=1-1

The Ghost at Beaverhead Rock. Returning home to his family in Alder Gulch, Dan discovers that Martha's first husband has been found murdered, and he is accused of being the killer.

https://www.amazon.com/Ghost-Beaverhead-Rock-Vigilante-Quartet-ebook/dp/B01GTZ4PZ0/ref=sr_1_3?keywords=the+Ghost+at+beaverhead+rock&qid=1571409478&s=books&sr=1-3

These books and others based on Montana's history, are available in both print and Kindle on Amason.com.

Subscribe to my newsletter, Montana's Vigilante History, for exclusive historical narratives about Montana's Vigilantes, and other events in our early history.

Go to https://carol-buchanan.com to sign up.

There you will also find my blog: "Montana's Storied Past": https://carol-buchanan.com/blog

I'll teach "Becoming Montana – Against the Odds" at Flathead Valley Community College (Continuing Education division) in the spring of 2021. Between 1857 and 1867, the pathway to becoming a Territory (the interim phase of becoming a state) was strewn with no-show judges, disappearing governors, and extreme lawlessness in the midst of a vacuum of law and a gold rush that rivalled California's 1849 rush for gold. Yet the pioneers of what became Montana persevered.

ABOUT CAROL BUCHANAN

Carol Buchanan writes historical fiction set in Montana, including a series about the Vigilantes of Montana, who battled terror on the roads during the Civil War, when gold, greed, and a vacuum of law led to ruffians' rule and a tolerance for murder. She has won both Spur and Spur Finalist awards. In 2001, she received a Washington State Top Ten Finalist award for Wordsworth's Gardens. In 2016, the Whitefish Library Association awarded her the "Spirit of Dorothy Johnson" award for her historical writing about Montana. A PhD in English & History, she teaches "Becoming Montana – Against the Odds," the early history of her home state, at Flathead Valley Community College in Kalispell, Montana. She enjoys reading, hiking, and watching movies with Richard, her husband of 40+ years. Her website is https://carol-buchanan.com.

Made in the USA
Middletown, DE
11 July 2021